# ALIENS IN THE HOUSE

## WRITTEN BY SUE BEHRENT
## ILLUSTRATED BY HEATH MCKENZIE

Published by Pearson Education Limited, 80 Strand, London, WC2R 0RL.

www.pearsonschools.co.uk

First published in 2010 by Pearson Australia.
This edition of *Aliens in the House* is published by Pearson Education Limited
by arrangement with Pearson Australia. All rights reserved.

Text © Pearson Australia 2010
Text by Sue Behrent

Original illustrations © Pearson Australia 2010
Illustrated by Heath McKenzie

22 21 20 19 18
10 9 8 7 6 5 4 3 2 1

**British Library Cataloguing in Publication Data**
A catalogue record for this book is available from the British Library

ISBN 978 0 435 19420 8

Printed in China by Golden Cup

**Acknowledgements**
We would like to thank the following schools for their invaluable help in the
development and trialling of the Bug Club resources: Bishop Road Primary
School, Bristol; Blackhorse Primary School, Bristol; Hollingwood Primary School,
West Yorkshire; Kingswood Parks Primary, Hull; Langdale CE Primary School,
Ambleside; Pickering Infant School, Pickering; The Royal School, Wolverhampton;
St Thomas More's Catholic Primary School, Hampshire; West Park Primary School,
Wolverhampton.

**Note from the publisher**
Pearson has robust editorial processes, including answer and fact checks, to ensure
the accuracy of the content in this publication, and every effort is made to ensure
this publication is free of errors. We are, however, only human, and occasionally
errors do occur. Pearson is not liable for any misunderstandings that arise as a
result of errors in this publication, but it is our priority to ensure that the content
is accurate. If you spot an error, please do contact us at resourcescorrections@
pearson.com so we can make sure it is corrected.

# CONTENTS

# CHAPTER 1
# UNDER ATTACK!

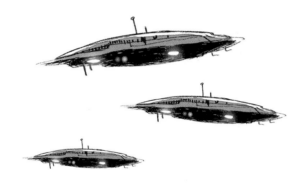

I was on my computer, playing a game called *Earth Under Attack*, when the news came through about a real alien invasion. I'm not kidding! I could hear it on the TV in the lounge. At first, I thought perhaps it was a science fiction show.

Mum and Dad were watching the TV and whispering. Of course, that made me suspicious.

"What's going on?" I asked them, standing by the living room door.

"**A-A-ALIENS,**" stuttered Mum in horror.

"**I-I-INVADING,**" stammered Dad in terror.

"What?" I asked, closing my eyes and opening them again. I felt like I was still playing the computer game. "You're joking, aren't you?"

"*No!*" said Mum and Dad at exactly the same time.

The worried looks on their faces convinced me. I sat down in front of the TV. The general in command of the armed forces was telling everyone to stay at home.

"I repeat, please do not go outside unless it's an emergency," said the general. "Families should stay inside and lock themselves in."

Suddenly, Mum gasped.

"*Nan!*" she half-whispered, her hand clamped over her mouth. "She's all alone in her flat! I'll have to go and get Nan and bring her back here."

"You heard the general," said Dad.

"He said no one was to go outside unless it was an emergency. Anyway, if anyone's going, it'll be me!" Dad folded his arms as if that settled the matter.

"This *is* an emergency!" Mum replied. "She's my mum, so I'm going to get her. Anyway, Doug, with your bad eyesight, you'd never make it to Nan's house in one piece!"

Dad pushed his glasses up his nose. He peered at Mum through the thick lenses. I could see Mum's point. Dad's eyesight is pretty bad, especially at night.

"Right, that's settled," said Mum quickly.

"Doug, you stay here and make sure no one can get in." She turned to look at me. "Baxter, you look after your little brother. He's asleep in his room, but if he wakes up, don't tell him about the aliens. He's too young to understand what's going on. He'll be frightened!"

Mum's voice wobbled. She looked as if she was about to cry.

"It's okay, Mum, I won't say a word," I promised.

"Good boy," she said. "Oh, and another thing. While Dad's outside making the house safe, don't open the door unless you can see that it's one of us. Okay?"

"All right, don't worry!" I said, getting a bit cross. "Just go and get Nan. We'll be fine!"

"I'll come out to the garage and check it's all safe out there. Then I can start locking all the doors and windows," Dad said to Mum, almost pushing her out of the door.

As I put the chain on the door, I heard the car tyres squeal and Mum sped off.

# CHAPTER 2
# JUSTIN WANTS TO KNOW ...

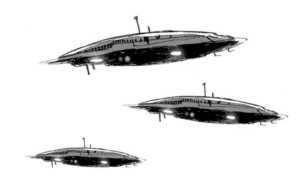

"Where are Mum and Dad?" asked a small voice behind me.

I almost jumped out of my skin in fright. I spun around to see Justin, my six-year-old brother, standing in the hallway.

"Mum's gone over to Nan's. Dad's
checking everything's safe outside,"
I said. "They'll be back soon."

"Mum's gone to Nan's? But it's …"
Justin looked up at the clock on the wall,
forgetting that he couldn't tell the time yet.
"… late," he finished.

"Yes it is, so what are you doing out
of bed?" I asked.

"I wanted to ask you something," said Justin softly.

"Okay, go back to bed. I'll be there in a minute," I replied.

Justin ran to his bedroom. I went into the lounge and turned down the TV. I'm not ashamed to admit that I checked the front door lock again. *Better safe than sorry,* I thought to myself as I peeped through the window at the night sky.

I went into Justin's room. He was sitting up in bed hugging his Captain Ooling toy. It was a character from his favourite cartoon, *Planetary Quest*.

"Do you believe in creatures from outer space?" Justin asked as I sat down on his bed.

"Did you have a bad dream?" I said, trying to change the subject.

The last thing I needed was Justin asking questions about aliens!

"No, silly," said Justin. "I just want to know. Do you think there are creatures living on other planets?"

I rolled my eyes. At least once a month Justin asks someone in the family whether they believe in aliens. He's obsessed with space travel! Nan is just as bad. She's always buying him books and posters about the galaxy and stuff.

When I ask Mum why, she just says, "Because that's what nans do!"

Although Justin can't tell the time, he does know a lot about the solar system. And he's pretty good at computer games too – for a little kid.

"Yeah, sure. I believe in aliens," I replied, trying to sound cool. Inside my head, my brain was yelling *YES! I BELIEVE IN ALIENS, BECAUSE THEY'RE HERE, RIGHT NOW!*

"Good, me too," replied Justin. He yawned and cuddled Captain Ooling.

"Okay, now why don't you go to sleep," I said.

"Night-night, Baxter," he murmured as I tiptoed out of his room. I closed the door and raced back to the lounge.

# CHAPTER 3
# YOU'RE NOT THE BOSS OF ME!

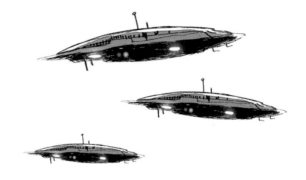

On the TV screen there were images of huge metal spaceships flying over famous landmarks. I turned up the sound a little to hear what was happening. I flicked through the channels.

"Buckingham Palace seems to be a meeting place for the space invaders," said one news reporter. Click.

"Here in Paris, the alien spaceships are floating above the Eiffel Tower," said another reporter. Click.

"As you can see, Martians are hovering over the Empire State Building in New York City," said a third reporter.

"Only stupid people would call them Martians," said a soft voice behind me. "Martians come from Mars."

For the second time that night, I jumped in fright! I'd been watching the TV so closely that I hadn't heard Justin come in.

"What are you doing back out of bed?" I snapped.

But Justin ignored me. He just stared at the TV.

"Justin, are you listening to me?" I growled, standing between him and the TV screen.

Justin frowned up at me.

"You're not the boss of me!" he yelled, suddenly. He rushed out of the lounge and up the hallway. I heard a door slam shut.

I should have followed Justin to his room and said sorry for getting angry. After all, the poor kid had just seen alien spaceships flying through the air. But I couldn't tear myself away from the TV!

"Spaceships are now pouring into Manchester. So far, no laser shots have been fired," said the news reporter.

Then it hit me. In all the news reports I'd seen, I hadn't heard anything about the aliens *attacking* anyone.

*That's weird*, I thought. If aliens were going to bother coming all this way, you'd think they'd try to conquer us! Maybe there would be more news on the internet.

I raced to my room to jump on the computer, but Justin had beaten me to it!

"What are you doing in here?" I asked. This time I really was angry.

"Playing *Earth Under Attack*," said Justin. His eyes were glued to the screen.

"Well, you'd better go back to bed," I said crossly. "This is my room and I need to use the internet."

But Justin still ignored me.

"I'm telling Dad – he's just outside, you know," I said, losing my cool.

"Do it, then!" Justin snapped back.

Something very weird was going on. Justin didn't seem like his normal self at all! Usually, Justin would never answer me back like that.

# CHAPTER 4
# THE VISITORS

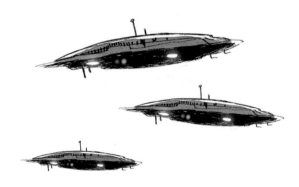

"You're going to–" I started to say.
Suddenly, a bright white light streamed
in through my bedroom window.

"What's that?" I yelled.

"It's the aliens! It's the aliens!"
chanted Justin.

He bounced up and down on my desk chair.

"Are you crazy?" I shouted. "Get under the bed, quick!"

But Justin hadn't listened to me before, and he wasn't about to start now. I watched in horror as he ran to the window.

"Get away from there!" I screamed. I dived at Justin to snatch him away from the window.

Then I remembered that Dad was still out there, checking the house was safe.

The bright beams of light hit me in the face as I grabbed Justin around the waist. Suddenly, the lights went out.

"The aliens are here! The aliens are here!" Justin shouted. Then we both heard a familiar sound.

The sound of car doors being slammed.

"Those beams of light," I said. "They weren't from a spaceship. They were from the headlights of Mum's car."

"The aliens are here!" Justin kept repeating. He was getting annoying.

"No, Justin, it's just Mum. She's home with Nan," I explained. "She'll be coming through the door any moment, just you wait and see."

"What's that then?" Justin said, pointing out of the window.

"Huh?" I looked up. The sky was filled with hovering lights, each one a different colour.

I let go of Justin and threw open the window.

"Quick, Mum, Dad, the aliens are coming!" I screamed. The lights in the sky grew larger as the spaceships approached.

"Open the front door," yelled Mum. "We'll never get Nan through your bedroom window!"

I ran down the hall, ripped the chain off the latch and flung open the door. Mum, Dad and Nan stumbled inside.

Dad slammed the door behind them, turned the lock, and leaned against the wall.

"We made it!" he said.

"So did we!" said a strange alien voice. Mum, Dad and I turned to see where the mysterious voice had come from. It didn't sound human!

All we saw was Nan, crouching down beside Justin, giving him a big hug.

"We did make it, didn't we Justin?" the raspy voice said again.

This time I watched in horror. Nan's lips had moved in time with the words.

"W-W-What's going on here?" Mum asked. Her voice was shaking with fear. She snatched Justin away by his arm.

"Why are you talking like that?" Mum asked Nan.

I was wondering the same thing. It was almost as if someone else was talking through Nan's mouth!

CHAPTER 5

# NOTHING IS AS IT SEEMS

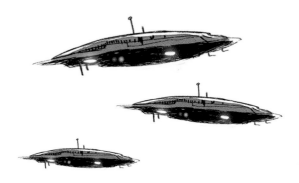

"Your mother and your son Justin are quite all right," said a different strange voice. But this voice wasn't coming from Nan. This time it was Justin's mouth that moved!

It was beginning to look as though both Justin and Nan had been taken over by aliens. But how? And more importantly, how were we going to get the real Nan and Justin back?

"We have been hiding inside Nan and Justin's bodies," said the voice coming from Justin's mouth.

"But now we are ready to go back in our spaceships to Raldo, our home planet," added Nan (or Alien-Nan).

For a moment, no one said anything. Mum and Dad stared in shock at Justin. I stood gaping at Nan.

"How long have you been ... er ... hiding?" I asked, backing away slightly.

"For hundreds of years," replied Alien-Justin.

"You can't have been hiding inside Nan and Justin for hundreds of years! Even Nan isn't *that* old!" I scoffed, which made Dad laugh.

"Well, obviously, we haven't been hiding in the same bodies for hundreds of years," sighed Alien-Justin. For a split second, he sounded just like my ordinary little brother.

"We were brought to your planet to observe how Earthlings work together and have fun together," explained Alien-Nan. "We didn't want to scare you, so we hid inside special people. We thought these people would help us with our plans."

I laughed. "Justin and Nan aren't special." Mum shot me an angry look.

"I mean, they're special to us ... but what use would they be to aliens?" I said.

"Two years ago, our leaders saw Justin and Nan playing spacemen in the park. Do you remember?" Alien-Nan turned to Alien-Justin and smiled. "I was Captain Ooling and you were Pring, Captain Ooling's partner."

"No, I'm pretty sure *I* was Captain Ooling ..." replied Alien-Justin with a frown.

"Er … *hello* … it doesn't really matter who played Captain Ooling," I snapped. "Just tell us why your leaders picked on Nan and Justin."

"Because they were having lots of fun," said Alien-Nan.

"Okay then," said Dad. "So why would you want to know about us Earthlings, anyway?"

"We have the power to travel into the future and back into the past," said Alien-Justin. "Fifty Earth years ago, one of our people called Sanoot travelled seventy Earth years into the future. He discovered something shocking."

Alien-Justin stopped. Alien-Nan took over the story.

"Sanoot learned that Earthlings would be frightened of us. They would try to attack our planet. We do not want this to happen," said Alien-Nan quietly.

"So you came here to destroy our planet first?" cried Mum.

"No. We came to learn how to make friends," said Alien-Justin.

# CHAPTER 6

# SAVING THE BIGGEST SURPRISE FOR LAST

"We came here to find out how we could get Earthlings to like us," added Alien-Nan. "So you wouldn't try to destroy us."

"Well, sending alien spaceships is hardly going to help!" said Dad.

"You do not understand," said Alien-Nan. "Our spaceships have come in peace! We are ready to return home. We now know how to make you Earthlings like us."

"Oh yeah?" said Dad. "How?"

"By being kind to everyone," said Alien-Justin. "And by being very, very good at computer games."

"What?" we all asked at once.

"Yes. In the future, there will be no need for war!" explained Alien-Justin. "Instead, players from both sides will see who can get the highest score in *Zoptal – Warrior Princess*."

We must have looked confused.

"It's a computer game that hasn't been invented yet, in your world-time," explained Alien-Nan.

"Er ... actually ... Nan? This whole time travelling thing is a bit confusing for us Earthlings," I began.

Alien-Nan smiled at me, so I continued.

"Fifty years ago, this Sanoot guy travelled seventy years into the future. So that's–" I counted up in my head, "twenty years from now, right?"

"You are correct," replied Alien-Nan with a nod.

"So, in twenty years, Earth would have been at war with your planet. But now, all that has changed because you beamed down a couple of aliens to take over the bodies of my family members?" I asked.

"Exactly," said my brother, now Alien-Justin. Then he looked at the clock. (Perhaps he *could* tell the time!) "We must leave you now," he said.

Suddenly, a red ball of energy shot out of his mouth. It hung in the air for a few seconds, and disappeared.

Justin's body shook. He opened his eyes and looked around, confused.

"Are you all right, darling?" Mum asked. She gave him a big sloppy kiss on the cheek.

Justin rubbed his eyes. Then he frowned and rubbed his cheek where Mum had kissed him. He was back to normal.

"Whoa! That was so weird!" I said.
Then I turned to Alien-Nan.

"I will miss you, Baxter," said Alien-Nan
with a wink. "You were clever enough to
teach your brother all the shortcuts and
cheats in *Earth Under Attack*. That will
come in very handy when he invents *Zoptal
– Warrior Princess*."

"What? You mean Justin is going to
invent *Zoptal – Warrior Princess*?" I asked.

Before Alien-Nan could answer, a distant
echoey voice spoke.

"Come on, Zoptal! Our spaceship is
waiting," said the voice. (It still sounded an
awful lot like Justin.)

Alien-Nan – Zoptal – grinned at me.
Then a small blue ball of energy floated
slowly out of her mouth and disappeared.

With a shudder, Nan opened her eyes and
smiled at us all.

"Shall I put the kettle on for a nice cup of tea?" she asked in her usual Nan voice.

At the window, we all peered into the dark, empty night sky.

"Well, that was a bit weird, wasn't it, Justin?" I said, turning to my brother. But Justin wasn't there. He'd already run back into my bedroom and was turning on the computer. The cheek of it! Still, I suppose he *did* have a computer game to invent ...